'Don't let fear hold you back.
You're **braver** than you think!'

Join Kitty for an enchanting
adventure by the light of the **moon**.

Kitty can **talk to animals** and
has **feline super-powers**.

Meet Kitty & her Cat Crew

Kitty

Kitty has special powers but is she ready to be a superhero just like her mum?

Luckily Kitty's Cat Crew have faith in her and show Kitty the hero that lies within!

Pumpkin

A stray ginger kitten who is utterly devoted to Kitty.

Figaro

Excitable and ready for adventure, Figaro knows
the neighbourhood like the back of his paw.

Pixie

Pixie has a nose for trouble
and a very active imagination!

Katsumi

Sleek and sophisticated,
Katsumi is quick to call Kitty
at the first sign of trouble.

For Emmeline. Welcome, little bean. – P.H

For Mum and her green thumb. – J.L

OXFORD
UNIVERSITY PRESS

Great Clarendon Street, Oxford OX2 6DP

Oxford University Press is a department of the University of Oxford.
It furthers the University's objective of excellence in research, scholarship, and
education by publishing worldwide. Oxford is a registered trade mark of Oxford
University Press in the UK and in certain other countries

British Library Cataloguing in Publication Data

Data available

ISBN: 978-0-19-277167-4

1 3 5 7 9 10 8 6 4 2

Printed in China

Paper used in the production of this book is a natural,
recyclable product made from wood grown in sustainable forests.
The manufacturing process conforms to the environmental
regulations of the country of origin.

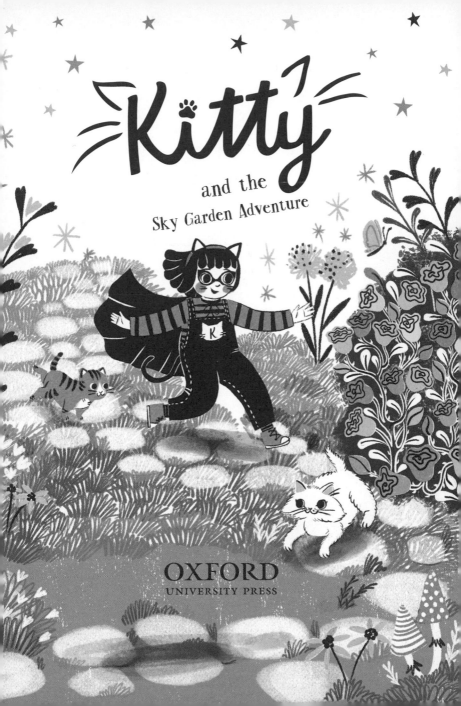

Chapter 1

'Look at this, Pumpkin.
My sunflower's starting to grow!' Kitty
gazed at the small plant in its little
brown pot. She was sitting on the flat
rooftop above her bedroom while
the stars appeared one by one in the

evening sky.

'It's got two leaves already!' said
Pumpkin, a roly-poly ginger kitten with
big blue eyes.

Kitty touched the sunflower's
sturdy stem and pointed leaves.
'I'm definitely putting sunflowers
into my design for

the new school garden. I just wish I
had a few more ideas . . .' She frowned
thoughtfully.

Kitty had been delighted when
her teacher had told the whole class
about the competition to design the
new school garden. All they had to do

was draw their plan for the garden on a piece of paper and colour it in carefully.

Her teacher had also said they could try growing a plant for the garden right away. Kitty had chosen a sunflower because she loved their beautiful round faces and flame-like petals. Kitty gazed at the sunflower and tried to imagine a new school garden. It was hard to know where to begin.

Darkness
had fallen and a
bright full moon hung in
the sky, pouring silvery light
over the houses. The streetlamps
of Hallam City winked below them
and in the distance an
owl hooted.

Kitty loved being out in the moonlight. She had special cat-like superpowers so she could easily climb and balance on the rooftops. Her night vision let her see in the dark, and her super hearing picked up sounds from a long way away.

She felt at home up here

and, when the moon came out, the world became shiny and magical. She loved sharing this special world with Pumpkin, the ginger kitten she'd rescued from the clock tower many weeks ago.

Kitty leaned in to look more closely at the sunflower plant. The night wind blew gently across the rooftop, making the plant's leaves flutter. There was the soft sound of paws padding over the roof tiles. Kitty listened carefully, 'Pixie, is that you?'

'You guessed right!' A fluffy white cat with green eyes sprang out from behind a chimney pot. Her pale fur gleamed in the moonlight. 'How did you know it was me?'

'I used my super hearing. Your paw steps sound lighter than Figaro's and quicker than Katsumi or Cleo's.' Kitty smiled. She had lots of good friends among the cats of Hallam City and meeting up with them on the rooftops was one of her favourite things to do.

'Hello, Pixie!' Pumpkin scampered

up to the white cat and they touched

noses. 'Have you come to play with us?'

'Yes, I was looking for something to

do,' admitted Pixie. 'I felt like having an

adventure and I thought to myself: who

would be the best person to have an

adventure with? Kitty, of course!'

Kitty laughed. 'That's very kind of you! I'm just trying to decide what to put in my design for the new school garden. I'd love to win the competition but I'm not sure what to draw.'

Pixie blinked thoughtfully and swished her snowy tail. 'I've heard of a place across the city with an amazing rooftop garden. Everyone knows about it but no one ever goes there because the old cat who guards the rooftop is so fierce. Maybe we could creep up to take a look. It might give you some ideas for designing your school garden.'

'But what if the old cat catches us?'
Pumpkin's whiskers quivered.

'We'll have to be quiet and sneaky.
That's what makes it an adventure!'
Pixie jumped on to the chimney
pot, her green eyes glittering with
excitement. 'It's not far away so we
could get there in a whisker!'

'I'd love to see this garden!' Kitty
glanced down at her pyjamas. 'But I'm
not really dressed for an adventure. Just
one second!'

She darted down the sloping roof and slipped through her bedroom window. Taking her black superhero suit from the wardrobe, she quickly pulled it on. Then she added her velvety cat ears and tied the dark, silky cape around her neck.

The moonlight poured over Kitty as she climbed over the windowsill. She felt her superpowers grow stronger and her body tingled from her head down to her toes. Her eyesight became clearer

and her hearing sharpened. Climbing to the top of the roof, she smiled at Pixie and Pumpkin. 'I'm ready now—let's go!'

They ran along the rooftop
together. Kitty beamed as she jumped
from one building to the next, her black
cape flying out behind her. She loved
the feel of the night breeze on her face
and the way the moonlight shimmered
on the windows.

The breeze grew stronger, rocking the trees in the park as they passed by. Pixie led them past Kitty's school with its square playground and climbing frame. Kitty spotted her table and chair through the classroom window. A pile of neatly sharpened pencils lay on the teacher's desk ready for the next day.

On the street behind the school there was a building site for a row of new houses. At the corner of the site, the builders had left a large skip full of odds and ends they were throwing away.

Every now and then Pixie stopped to sniff the air. 'Yes, it's this way,' she called to the others. 'I can smell the scent of flowers.'

Kitty smiled. 'I can smell them too!' The sweet smell drifting on the night breeze reminded her of roses.

One by one they jumped from the rooftop to the ledge of an apartment building. Then Pixie led them up the steps of the fire escape. The scent of

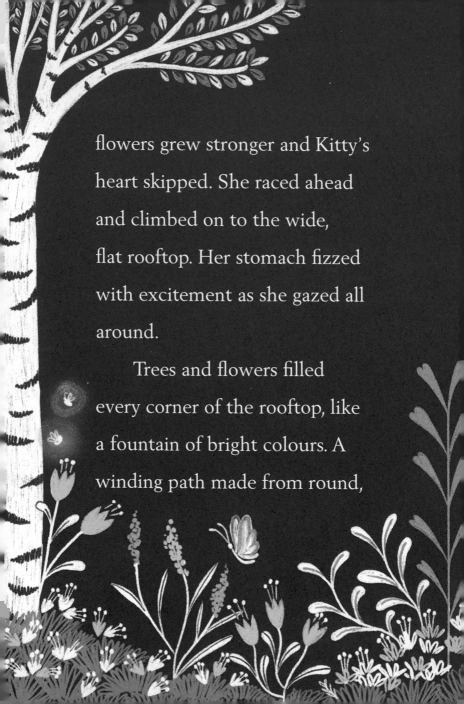

flowers grew stronger and Kitty's
heart skipped. She raced ahead
and climbed on to the wide,
flat rooftop. Her stomach fizzed
with excitement as she gazed all
around.

Trees and flowers filled
every corner of the rooftop, like
a fountain of bright colours. A
winding path made from round,

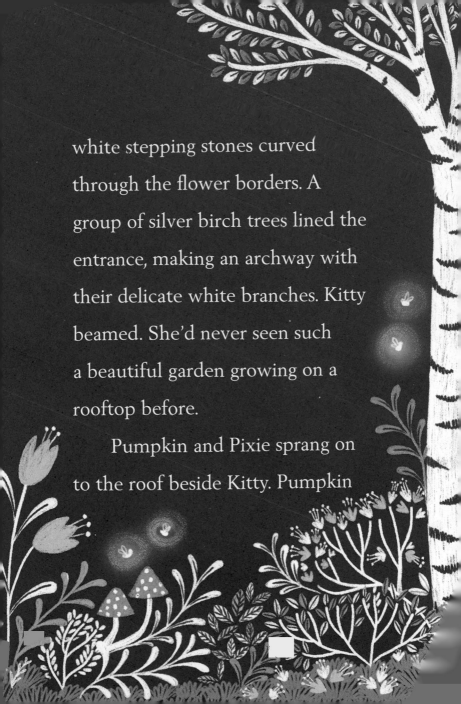

white stepping stones curved through the flower borders. A group of silver birch trees lined the entrance, making an archway with their delicate white branches. Kitty beamed. She'd never seen such a beautiful garden growing on a rooftop before.

Pumpkin and Pixie sprang on to the roof beside Kitty. Pumpkin

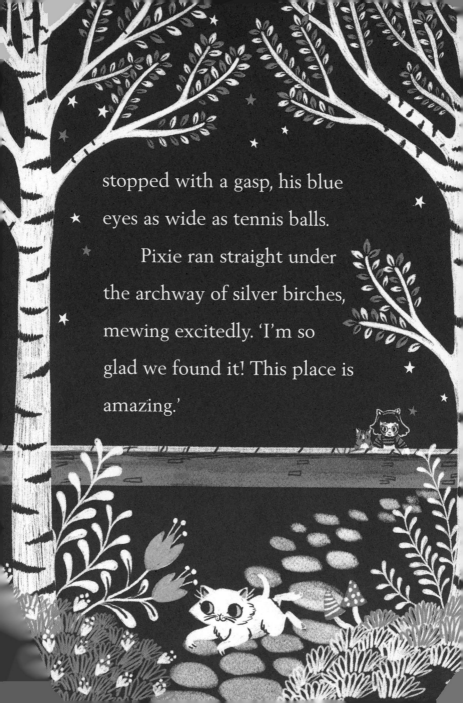

stopped with a gasp, his blue
eyes as wide as tennis balls.

Pixie ran straight under
the archway of silver birches,
mewing excitedly. 'I'm so
glad we found it! This place is
amazing.'

'It's wonderful!' Kitty stepped under the archway of trees. Gazing upwards, she saw the stars sparkling brightly through the web of branches and leaves. She walked on and a cluster of tall, bright sunflowers caught her eye. She stopped beside the towering plants. 'Look at these sunflowers! They're the biggest ones I've ever seen.'

There were seven sunflowers altogether, each one taller than Kitty, and they nodded their heads gently in the breeze. She gazed at them

admiringly and their cheerful faces seemed to smile down at her. She reached up to touch the nearest flower. The golden petals were silky smooth around the rough, black centre.

Kitty tingled with excitement. There was something special about this garden. The plants were so perfect they looked as if they were grown with magic!

Chapter 2

Kitty pulled herself away
from the amazing sunflowers and
followed the winding path. She stopped
for a moment to look for the fierce,
old cat that guarded the place but the
sky garden seemed to be empty.

Pixie scampered after her, swishing her tail with excitement.

Pumpkin hid behind the sunflowers. 'Are you sure we're safe?'

'I don't think anyone else is here,' said Kitty. 'Come and look, Pumpkin. This place is lovely!'

'It's more than lovely,' mewed Pixie. 'It's magnificent! And it smells like heaven.'

Kitty passed a yellow rose bush growing beside a pink rose bush. She leaned in to sniff them. 'These roses

smell wonderful. Which ones do you like best?'

Pixie and Pumpkin didn't reply so
Kitty turned round to look for them.
The little white cat and the ginger kitten
were taking it in turns to leap into the
middle of a purple-flowered bush and
roll from side to side with their paws
in the air.

'What are you doing?' cried Kitty.
'This isn't our garden!'

'It's a catnip plant, Kitty,' giggled
Pixie. 'I just can't help it!'

'Whee!' said Pumpkin, jumping
into the bush and rolling around again.

Kitty hurried across to the catnip bush. She'd heard of a plant that cats loved but she hadn't realized it could make them act so silly. 'Stop, Pumpkin! Stop it, Pixie!' she told her friends. 'What if the owner of the garden comes along?'

'What's going on here?' said a deep voice. 'None of you should be in this garden. Don't you know you're trespassing?'

Kitty's tummy lurched guiltily. Turning round, she spotted a huge

shadow with pointy ears on the wall.
She gulped. Was it the fierce old cat
that guarded the rooftop? Pumpkin
squeaked with fright and hid behind
Kitty's legs.

'I'm extremely disappointed that
you came in without even asking,'
growled the voice.

'You're right—we should have
asked! We heard how lovely the garden
was and we wanted to see the place for
ourselves.' Kitty peered through the
cluster of plants.

There was the sound of paws padding through the undergrowth and an old tortoiseshell cat with grey whiskers appeared. He twitched his ears disapprovingly. Pixie leapt out of the catnip bush and began grooming her tail, pretending that she'd been behaving sensibly all along.

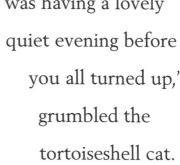

'I was having a lovely quiet evening before you all turned up,' grumbled the tortoiseshell cat.

'I'm sorry—we didn't mean to disturb you,' said Kitty. 'My name's Kitty and this is Pixie and Pumpkin.' The tortoiseshell cat was still frowning, so she carried on, hurriedly, 'Do you live here with your owner?'

'That's right.' The tortoiseshell studied each of them suspiciously. 'I'm Diggory and my human, Mrs Lovett, created this whole place. She's spent years getting it perfect so I shan't let you young rascals come along and ruin it all!'

'We only came to take a peek at the place. You see—I've got to draw a design for a new school garden,' explained Kitty. 'I'm sorry my friends were a bit silly when they smelt the catnip bush.'

'We're really sorry!' Pixie blurted out.

Pumpkin hung his head and stared at the stepping stones.

'Well, I suppose the catnip bush is quite exciting,' Diggory said slowly. 'It sends us silly—like humans when they eat too many sweets. I'm a bit too old to roll around in it these days, though.'

Kitty smiled. The old cat was a little gruff at first but he wasn't as fierce as Pixie had described. 'So do you think we could look around for a little longer?' she asked, shyly. 'We'll be careful around the plants, I promise. It's just such an amazing place—I would love to see the rest of it.'

'We're not really accustomed to having visitors. It can get a little lonely at times and it's hard to manage looking after the garden with just the two of us,' Diggory told them. 'It would be nice to share the place with someone

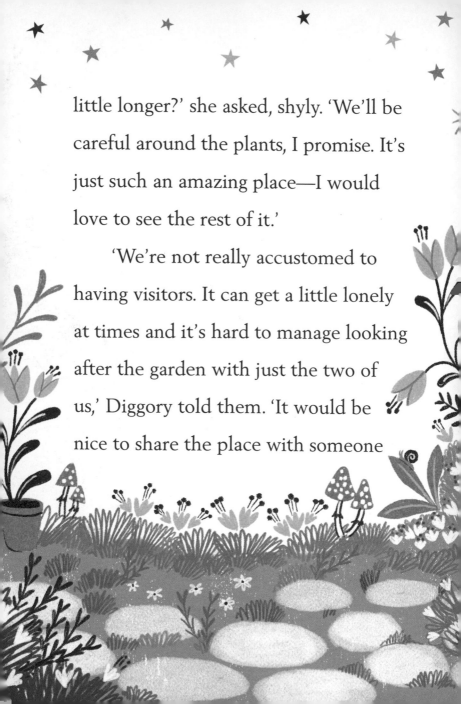

who's interested in the plants.' He
turned slowly and led them down the
stepping stones.

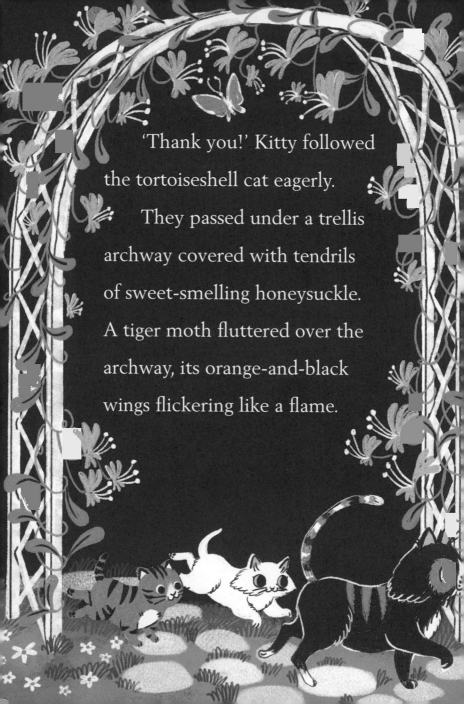

'Thank you!' Kitty followed
the tortoiseshell cat eagerly.

They passed under a trellis
archway covered with tendrils
of sweet-smelling honeysuckle.
A tiger moth fluttered over the
archway, its orange-and-black
wings flickering like a flame.

Diggory stopped beside a beautiful bench decorated with carved wooden leaves. He waved a paw at a cluster of white star-shaped flowers growing beside it. They glowed brightly like tiny lights. 'These spring stars are Mrs Lovett's favourite flowers. They remind her how much she likes to sit here and look at the stars from time to time.'

'What a lovely name!' Kitty looked up in surprise as music tinkled in the tree above her head. Hanging from a branch was a wind chime made from delicate seashells. The breeze ruffled the tree, making the wind chime sway. The musical notes drifted over the garden like a magical spell and the flowers seemed to lean towards the enchanting sound. Kitty's skin prickled as she listened, watching the dangling chime twist and turn. The shells' pearl-like sheen gleamed in the moonlight.

Diggory noticed Kitty's gaze. 'It's beautiful, isn't it? That wind chime is Mrs Lovett's pride and joy. She made it herself from seashells she gathered as

a little girl. I don't think
the garden would be the
same without it.'

Pixie leapt up
the tree to the branch
holding the wind chime
to take a closer look. 'It's so
pretty,' she mewed. 'Don't you think
it's shiny, Kitty?' She padded closer and
the branch began to bend under her
weight.

'Yes, I do . . . but I think you'd
better get down!' Kitty quickly climbed

on to the bench and steadied the
branch with her hand.

Pixie turned round and darted back
down the tree trunk. Diggory frowned
as the wind chime jangled alarmingly.
Kitty let go once the branch was steady.
Then she sat down on the wooden
bench and gazed at the amazing plants
all around her. Pumpkin leapt on to the
bench beside her, yawning, and curled
up with his furry head in her lap.

'There's so much to see!' Pixie
scampered up and down the winding

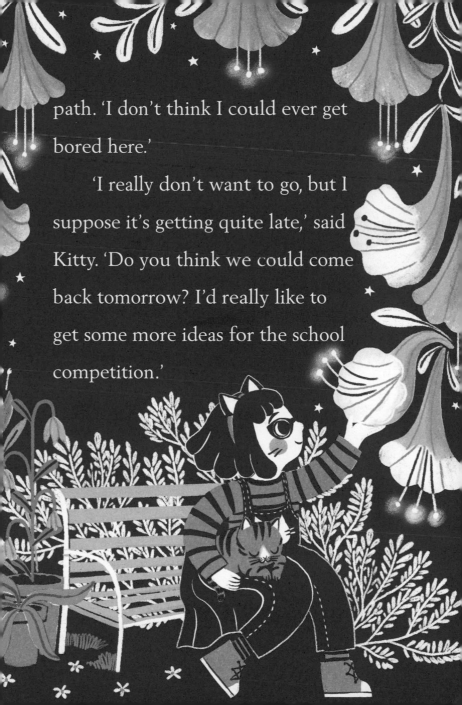

path. 'I don't think I could ever get bored here.'

'I really don't want to go, but I suppose it's getting quite late,' said Kitty. 'Do you think we could come back tomorrow? I'd really like to get some more ideas for the school competition.'

Diggory nodded. 'I'd forgotten how nice it is to show visitors around. You're welcome to come back, Kitty. I will look out for you.'

'Thank you!' Kitty smiled at the tortoiseshell cat. 'See you tomorrow.'

Pixie, Pumpkin, and Kitty made their way back through the archway of silver birch trees. Kitty took one final look at the sky garden before climbing on to the fire escape. The night breeze swept across the garden, rustling the leaves and making the

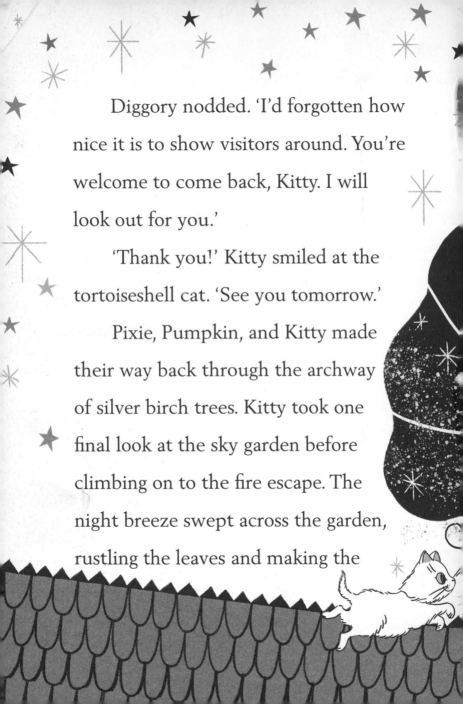

sunflowers nod their heads.

The wind chime twisted and turned, winking in the moonlight and playing its beautiful music. The magical sound cchoed around Kitty's head as she darted across the city rooftops and home to bed.

Chapter
3

The next evening, there
was a tapping on Kitty's bedroom
window just after moonrise. Kitty
opened the window and smiled. 'Hello,
Pixie! You're quite early tonight.'

'I love being early!' Pixie leapt

through the window, her green eyes gleaming. 'Shall we go back to the sky garden now? Wouldn't you like to get some more ideas for your garden design?'

'Yes I would! It's such a beautiful place.' Kitty turned to Pumpkin, who was lying on the bed with his stripy tail wrapped around his ginger tummy. 'Are you ready to go, Pumpkin?'

Pumpkin stretched his paws and yawned. 'I'm ready. I was just having a quick catnap!'

Kitty put on her cat superhero costume. Then she and Pixie climbed out of the window and up to the rooftop. The breeze ruffled Kitty's hair and made her cape swirl around her legs. Stars began appearing one by one like tiny sparks in the darkening sky. Pumpkin climbed after them, still yawning.

Pixie ran to the edge of the roof and sniffed the air eagerly. 'Come on—let's not waste any time!'

Kitty jumped to the next building, her cape flying out behind her. Pumpkin and Pixie padded after her. They ran along the rooftops and gazed down at the quiet streets below. When they passed the building site, Kitty spotted a pile of empty paint cans lying inside the rubbish skip. The metal cans glinted as the moon came out from behind a cloud.

Pixie streaked ahead, reaching the apartment building with the fire escape.

'Slow down, Pixie,' called Kitty,

laughing. 'You're as fast as a cheetah

tonight!'

'I can't help it!' Pixie's words

floated back to her. 'I'm too excited

to go any slower.'

Kitty stopped suddenly, her hand on the rail of the fire escape. There was a lot of mewing and yowling coming from the rooftop. She had been too busy talking to Pixie and Pumpkin to notice it before.

'Kitty, do you hear that?' Pumpkin shrank back. 'Maybe we shouldn't go up there.'

An ear-splitting screech cut through the night, followed by a burst of wild laughter.

A cold prickle ran down Kitty's neck. 'That sounds like it's coming from the sky garden!' She darted up the metal steps, trying to catch up with Pixie.

The little white cat hesitated at the edge of the rooftop. Her snowy tail flicked to and fro and she pinned her ears back in alarm.

'Pixie, what's wrong?' Kitty raced up the last few steps. Her heart sank as she reached the top and stared around the crowded garden.

There were cats everywhere—black ones, white ones, ginger, grey, and tabby. They were dashing along the paths, trampling over the flowerbeds, and pouncing on each other in the bushes. Three cats were climbing the archway of silver birch trees and several delicate white branches had already snapped off and fallen to the ground.

Diggory, the old tortoiseshell cat, was pacing up and down, shaking his head. His fur stood on end and his grey whiskers were shaking. 'Get down from there!' he mewed at one of the cats in the trees. 'Get your paws off that rose bush!' he snapped at another.

Pixie's tail swished nervously. She gazed around with wide, shocked eyes.

'Diggory, what's happening?' cried Kitty. 'Where did all these cats come from?'

'I don't know. They've been arriving for hours and they won't leave!' growled Diggory. 'They've torn down the fairy lights on the honeysuckle trellis and trodden on so many beautiful flowers. I knew it was a mistake to let visitors in here! When Mrs Lovett sees the garden she'll be heartbroken.'

'But why are they here? I thought people didn't really visit the garden.' Kitty noticed Pixie's ears were drooping. The little cat looked terribly guilty. 'Pixie, did you tell lots of cats about this place?'

Pixie nodded with a wailing meow. 'I'm REALLY sorry! I just was so excited after seeing this place that I told everyone how amazing it was and I said the cat who lived here wasn't scary at all! I didn't think they'd all rush over and ruin the garden.'

Diggory shook his head sadly. 'What am I supposed to do? These cats won't listen to me. Most of them have rolled in the catnip bush and nothing I say will stop their ridiculous behaviour!'

'We're so sorry, Diggory!' said Kitty, giving Pixie a stern look. 'We'll get these cats to leave before things get any worse. Pixie, you guard the catnip bush and don't let any cats touch it. Pumpkin and I will round them up and send them home.'

Kitty rushed over to a group of cats climbing all over the garden bench. She took a deep breath, saying firmly, 'It's time to go! And don't come back again unless Diggory invites you.'

A small tortoiseshell cat tried to

hide behind the honeysuckle vines.
'You're just a bossy boots!' she
shouted as Kitty shooed her out of her
hiding place.

'Be careful! That's the owner's
favourite flower,' Pumpkin cried, as a
black cat trampled right through the
spring stars bush.

A plump cat with thick,
grey fur and droopy whiskers

was perched halfway up the wind chime tree. 'Ooh, look! It's the Garden Police! Why are you making such a fuss, you silly girl? We're only having a bit of fun.' He fixed Kitty with his cold blue eyes and flexed his sharp claws. The tree branch rocked and the wind chime jangled.

'Your fun is ruining the garden!' said Kitty. 'And please don't damage that wind chime. It's very precious!'

The plump cat eyed the wind chime. Then he yawned, showing off his pointed teeth. 'You can't keep a special place like this all for yourself. It's very selfish!' He began grooming his long fur.

'Hey, Duke!' yelled a small tortoiseshell cat. 'Come and try out this catnip bush.'

The plump, grey cat waved at the other cat before turning back to Kitty. 'Don't you think you should learn to share a little? If you don't you could be very VERY sorry!'

Kitty frowned. 'Why? What do you mean . . .' She broke off and ran to help Pixie, who was struggling to keep cats away from the catnip bush. 'You'd better go quickly,' she told them. 'If the owner comes out you'll be in a lot of trouble.'

'Well the fun is CLEARLY over!' Duke climbed down from the wind chime tree and shook his long whiskers angrily. He glared at Kitty again before heading to the edge of the rooftop. When he snapped his claws, the other cats slunk after him, mumbling complaints.

'It's not fair!' cried the tortoiseshell cat. 'We were having a nice time before you came along.'

Kitty shook her head at the creature's rudeness. The cats crowded towards the fire escape, yelling at each other and trampling on the flower beds. At last they were gone.

A lump rose in Kitty's throat as she gazed around the sky garden. The place had looked so perfect yesterday evening. Crushed petals and torn leaves were scattered across the stepping

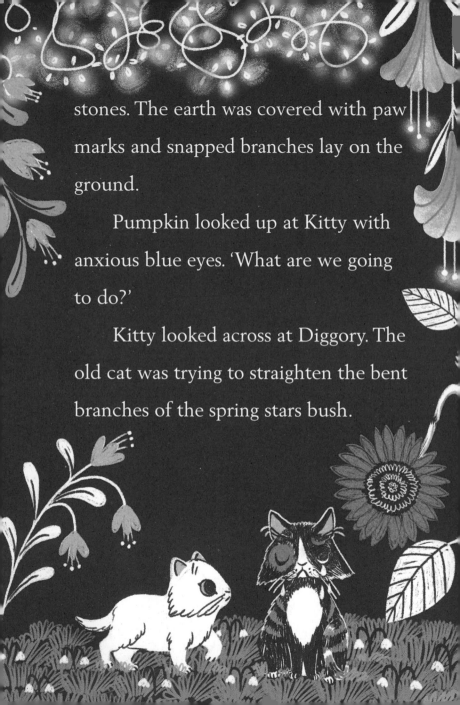

stones. The earth was covered with paw marks and snapped branches lay on the ground.

Pumpkin looked up at Kitty with anxious blue eyes. 'What are we going to do?'

Kitty looked across at Diggory. The old cat was trying to straighten the bent branches of the spring stars bush.

A large tear rolled down his furry face.
Kitty swallowed. 'We're going to
make this right! If we work hard as
a team we can put this garden back
together again.'

Chapter 4

Kitty dusted off her hands. 'We must fix this before morning! We can't let Mrs Lovett wake up and see the garden looking this way.'

Diggory shook his head. 'There's no need to do anything! I know you're

66

only trying to help, but Mrs Lovett and I always look after this garden by ourselves.'

Kitty crouched down beside Diggory. Her heart sank as she saw how tired and sad he looked. 'Please let us help! I promise we won't stop until the garden looks better again.'

'We could start by clearing up the

broken flowers and leaves,' suggested
Pumpkin.

Diggory frowned. 'Well, all right
then. I'll show you where the broom is.'
He led them to a small brown shed in
the corner of the rooftop.

Kitty took out a rake, a broom,
and some gardening gloves. She swept
along the stepping stones, while Pixie
and Pumpkin picked up the broken
flower stems and dropped them in the
composter. They raced up and down
the garden. Kitty's heart thumped. They

had to hurry if they were going to finish clearing up before sunrise!

Pixie and Pumpkin began tidying the fallen leaves. Kitty snipped some drooping stems off the rose bush and tied the climbing honeysuckle back on to the trellis. She watered each sunflower, as their leaves were drooping. One flower was broken beyond repair but the others seemed much better again.

'What shall we do about all these, Kitty?' Pumpkin pointed to a row of smashed plant pots with earth spilling out of the sides. The purple lavender growing in each one had a strong, sweet smell.

'We don't have any spare pots, I'm afraid.' Diggory shook his head. 'We'll have to throw away those lavenders.'

A determined look shone in Kitty's eyes. 'These flowers are much too

pretty to lose! We'll just have to find a few pots from somewhere.' She darted to the metal stairs, calling to Diggory, 'Don't worry—we'll be back soon!'

Pumpkin scampered after Kitty, with Pixie close behind.

'Where are we going?' Pixie waved her fluffy, white tail. 'None of the shops will be open, Kitty. We can't buy new plant pots till tomorrow morning.'

'I know—but that'll be too late!' Kitty rubbed her forehead worriedly. 'Maybe there's something else we can use. Let's look around and see.' She leapt to the roof next door before clambering down a drainpipe. Crossing the road carefully, she stopped beside the row of newly built houses.

A pile of empty paint cans lay at the top of the builder's rubbish skip. An idea popped into Kitty's head and she took out the paint cans and checked each one. 'These are clean and they're just the right size! I think they'll look lovely with flowers inside.'

'That's a great idea!'

mewed Pumpkin.

Pixie leapt on to the side of the
skip. 'How about this bucket? And
look—here's a pair of red wellies.
Would they look nice with plants
growing in them?'

'They'd look wonderful!' Kitty
beamed. 'All kinds of recycled things
will work as plant pots.' She gathered
up the bucket and the old boots and
carried them back to the rooftop.
Then she returned to fetch the
empty paint cans.

Working as fast as she could, Kitty
filled each container with earth. Then
one by one, she planted the flowers
inside them. Lavenders bloomed
from the paint cans and yellow tulips
sprouted from the old red boots. A
silver-winged moth fluttered through
the air and rested on a tulip, flexing its
delicate wings.

Kitty finished sweeping before climbing the trellis to hang the fairy lights back in place. Then she raked the flowerbed to get rid of all the paw prints. Pumpkin and Pixie tidied the fallen leaves off the stepping stones. Kitty's heart skipped as she gazed around. They'd finished repairing the garden before sunrise!

Pixie and Pumpkin sat on the bench for a rest while Kitty went to find Diggory. The old tortoiseshell cat was sitting beside a stone basin

filled with water, gazing at the moon's
reflection in the rippled surface. He
looked at Kitty mournfully. 'I guess
sweeping and tidying can't really make
up for all the damage that was done.'

'No, but we replaced the broken
pots and replanted all the flowers.

Come and see!' Kitty nervously led Diggory towards the centre of the garden. The recycled plant pots they had chosen were very different from the ones used before. She really hoped the old cat liked them!

Diggory followed Kitty around the garden. He listened carefully while she explained about re-using the paint cans and the wellington boots. Slowly, a warm smile grew on his face and his ears pricked up.

'So we hope you like what we've

done,' said Kitty shyly. 'We can change things back again if you don't.'

'No, you don't need to do that!' Diggory told her. 'I wouldn't have thought of it myself, but these recycled pots look wonderful.'

'That was all Kitty's idea!' Pumpkin put in.

Kitty brushed earth off her hands. She couldn't shake the feeling that something wasn't right. The garden didn't feel as magical somehow. The flowers didn't lean towards the centre of the garden the way they had before.

Diggory tottered towards the garden seat. A gust of wind swirled over the rooftop, rocking the tree behind the bench. Diggory stiffened and peered closely at the long branches. 'Nooo!' he yowled. 'It's gone! The beautiful wind chime is missing.'

Kitty gasped, staring at the empty branch. Where had the wind chime gone?

'Wait! Maybe it just fell to the ground.' Pixie jumped down from the bench to search the undergrowth.

Pumpkin joined her and they all hunted through the bushes. Kitty climbed the tree to check that the wind chime wasn't hanging on another branch, hidden by the leaves.

'One of those naughty cats must have taken it,' said Kitty at last.

'Maybe we can make a new one by re-using old things like we did with the plant pots,' said Pumpkin hopefully.

'That just won't do!' mewed Diggory. 'It isn't just any old wind chime. Mrs Lovett made it from seashells that she gathered as a child. All the love and care that went into making the wind chime turned it into something magical. I don't think the garden will grow the same without it.'

Kitty gazed around the sky garden. The flowers had lost their bright sheen and the trees rattled in the wind. Even the sunflowers bowed their heads sadly. The magic of the garden had vanished, like the moon hidden by a cloud.

'This is my fault!' Pixie's voice

trembled. 'I was the one that told all those careless cats about the garden.'

'I'll use my super hearing to find them,' said Kitty. 'They can't have gone very far.'

'Please be careful,' said Diggory. 'Goodness knows what those wild cats will do next!'

'Don't worry!' said Kitty. 'We've faced tricky adventures before. We'll search the city until we get the wind chime back again!'

Chapter
5

Kitty ran from one corner

of the rooftop to the next. She listened

desperately for the tinkling sound of

the wind chime. At first all she could

hear was the wind whistling round the

chimney pots. Then her super hearing

grew stronger and she caught a faint jingling noise.

'Pixie! Pumpkin! I think I can hear it.' Kitty raced over the rooftops. She sprang from one roof to another, turning a somersault as she leapt over a chimney pot.

As she ran, she strained to hear the distant sound of the wind chimes. Sliding down a drainpipe, Kitty followed the sound to an alleyway between two tall houses.

She crept to the edge of a roof

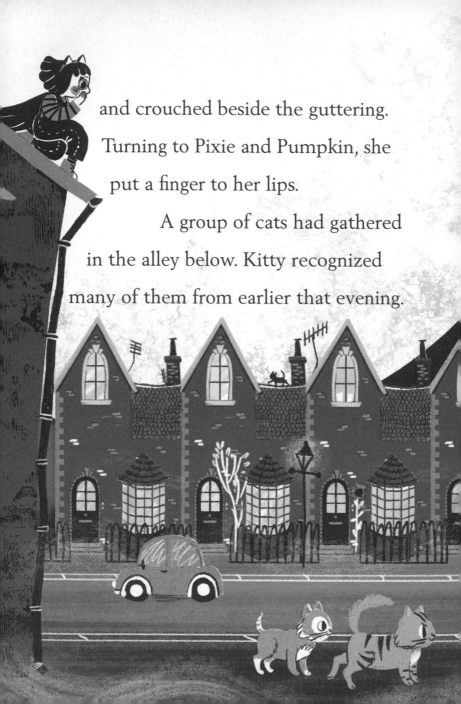

and crouched beside the guttering.
Turning to Pixie and Pumpkin, she
put a finger to her lips.

A group of cats had gathered
in the alley below. Kitty recognized
many of them from earlier that evening.

The group was crowding around Duke, the plump cat with the droopy whiskers, as he held the wind chime up in the air. The silvery seashells glinted in the moonlight.

'Now, listen!' Duke shook the wind chime roughly. 'I've had enough of all of your yowling.'

'But Duke!' whined a tall ginger cat. 'I was the one that sneaked that dangly thing out of the garden so I should get to keep it.'

'It should be mine! I carried

it all the way down the drainpipe,'
complained a black cat. 'You would
have lost it somewhere.'

'No, I wouldn't!' said the ginger cat
crossly.

More cats joined in, all mewing and
complaining at the same time.

'ENOUGH!' yelled Duke. 'If you
can't agree then we'll break it up and
have a piece each.'

Kitty gasped. How dare he think of
taking apart the magical wind chime?
Without it, the sky garden would never

be the same again. She couldn't let that happen!

'What shall we do, Kitty?' whispered Pumpkin.

'Leave it to me!' Kitty whispered back. 'I'm going down there.'

Duke began pulling the seashells off the string and throwing them to his gang.

Kitty's heart thumped as she looked at the alley below. The ground was a long way away but her superpowers would help her.

She balanced on the edge of the rooftop, spreading her cape with her hands. Taking a brave leap, she plunged through the air. 'Cat power!' she yelled as her cape flew out, slowing her fall.

She landed lightly in front of Duke, steadying herself with one hand on the alley wall.

'Look everyone!' sneered Duke, pulling more shells off the wind chime. 'It's the silly girl who chased us out of the sky garden.'

'Give those shells back!' cried
Kitty. 'The garden won't be the same
without the wind chime.'

'Tough luck!' Duke laughed nastily
and threw a shell to a black cat. 'Here—
catch Mungo.'

'Stop it!' Kitty leapt into the air,
reaching as high as she could, but the
shell sailed over her head.

Duke laughed even harder and
threw more shells through the air. Kitty
caught one but she missed the next and
chased after the tall ginger cat, who

scampered away down the
alley.

'We'll help you, Kitty!'
Pixie clambered down
the drainpipe followed by
Pumpkin.

Kitty, Pixie and
Pumpkin chased after the
gang of cats. Kitty dashed
to and fro, turning head
over heels to catch the
silvery shells. Soon she had
a handful tucked in her

pocket but Duke was still pulling more of them off the wind chime.

'There are too many cats and too many shells, Kitty!' panted Pumpkin.

Kitty paused to catch her breath. Tears pricked her eyes as she saw the empty strings dangling from the wind chime. There was no more beautiful tinkling sound, only the noise of the wind in the alley and Duke's laughter.

'You thought you could beat us, didn't you?' crowed Duke. 'But you're not fast enough to catch us all!'

Kitty gazed despairingly at the cat gang spread out along the alley. Suddenly she noticed a few of them shaking their seashells and frowning. Another cat was tapping his shell against the alley wall.

'It's not working anymore!' complained the tall ginger cat.

'Stupid shell!' said the black cat. 'Where's the tinkly noise gone?'

Kitty shook her head. 'The wind chime only makes a sound when the pieces are joined together,' she explained. 'Shaking one bit doesn't work! We have to put the shells back on the string again.'

The cat gang looked at each other uncertainly.

'Don't pay any attention to her!' growled Duke, but Kitty wasn't finished. She saw she had their attention and leapt up on to a bin so all the cats could see her. She had to make them understand!

'Listen, I know you were all really cross when I told you to leave the garden,' she went on. 'I am not a silly girl and you were wrong to mess around in the trees and the flowerbeds . . . but maybe we should have found a way to enjoy the place together.'

Some of the cats murmured and nodded.

Pixie's ears pricked up and she whispered, 'Keep going, Kitty! I think they're finally listening.'

'Why don't you come back there with me?' suggested Kitty. 'If you each say sorry to Diggory, the owner's cat, and give back your piece of the wind chime then I'll talk to him about letting you visit.'

'That's a stupid idea!' scoffed Duke. 'You'll have us singing songs to the moon next!'

The gang of cats gathered together, whispering and meowing.

'Hey!' Duke's whiskers quivered. 'You're not actually falling for this, are you?'

At last, a thin tabby cat with a crooked ear padded up to Kitty. 'We'll come with you and take our shells back where they belong.'

'That's awesome!' Kitty beamed and shook the tabby's paw. 'My name's Kitty. Anyone else who wants to do the right thing and return the wind chime should follow me. If we're quick we can get back to the sky garden before sunrise.'

A line of cats followed Kitty down the alley and on to the rooftop.

Duke yelled up at them as they trooped round the chimney pots. 'You're all being stupid! Cats are meant to be wild and naughty. Cats are meant to do whatever they like!'

'Be quiet, Duke!' the tabby called down. 'You're just cross because we're not doing what you want anymore.'

When Kitty reached the sky garden rooftop, she held up her hand to signal the cats to wait. Hurrying down the stepping stones, she found Diggory alone on the bench staring sadly at the stars.

'Those cats have come to apologize for all the trouble they caused,' she told Diggory.

The old cat scowled. 'After all they've done I'm surprised they dare to show their faces!'

'I know they were really naughty but they say they're sorry now. Wouldn't it be nice to have visitors in the garden sometimes?' Kitty noticed Diggory's tail twitch thoughtfully. 'They have all the shells for the wind chime so if you have some spare string we can fix the chime back together again.'

Diggory's ears pricked up. 'There's some string in the shed. I'll fetch it right now!'

Chapter 6

Kitty brought the cat gang

on to the rooftop and they lined up

along the stepping stones. Looking

round at the sky garden, they began

whispering to each other and pointing

to the flowers and the new plant pots.

'Did you do all this, Kitty?' asked the tall ginger cat. 'It looks so tidy.'

'My friends Pixie and Pumpkin helped too,' replied Kitty.

Diggory returned with some thick green string and the tabby cat with the crooked ear stepped forwards, looking very ashamed of herself. 'I'm truly sorry for spoiling your garden,' she mewed. 'I was horrible and selfish, and I promise I'll never do anything like it again.'

Diggory nodded. Taking her shell, he threaded it onto the first piece of string. After that each cat came up to apologize and add their shell to the string. Soon there were five long threads full of beautiful silvery shells.

When Diggory had finished arranging the shells, worry creased his whiskery face. 'Kitty, we're missing the piece in the middle that makes it chime.'

'Duke has that piece. I think he'll be here any minute.' Kitty crossed her fingers behind her back. She really hoped she was right and Duke came along with the missing piece soon!

Diggory sat on the bench, holding the strings of shells patiently. The cats gathered round him, gazing at the seashells as they twisted and turned in the night breeze.

Pixie and Pumpkin ran to the edge of the roof and peered at the street below.

'I can't see anyone coming,' called Pixie, sadly. 'No, wait!'

Pumpkin danced around in a circle. 'It's Duke! He's climbing up the

fire escape.'

Kitty held her breath as the
plump grey cat clambered on to
the rooftop. He stroked his whiskers
before clearing his throat. 'I'm . . . I'm

sorry I caused so much trouble,' he told Diggory, his tail drooping. 'Your garden is brilliant and I shouldn't have rushed in and spoiled it all.'

Diggory frowned before taking the chime from Duke's paws. 'Well, we all make mistakes from time to time,' he said slowly. 'Perhaps I could have invited visitors here sooner. So if you promise to keep to the paths and look after the plants then . . . you're welcome to stay.'

Duke clapped his paws together with excitement, before trying to act cool. 'Sure—I can promise all that! It looks nice now the place is tidy again.'

Diggory carefully tied the chime

between the strings of shells. Then
Kitty climbed the tree behind the
bench and hung the chime carefully
from a long branch. Everyone watched
and waited.

There was a moment of silence.
Then a breath of wind swirled over the
rooftop, making the seashells sway.

The wind chime tinkled softly and all the cats cheered.

Diggory smiled widely. 'This has been a night of surprises. Thank you, Kitty, for making me realize how much I've missed having visitors.' He clambered down from the bench. 'Now I'd better water the plants like I do every evening.'

'Why don't you sit and rest? We can finish the chores.' Duke clapped his paws. 'Right everyone, fill up the watering cans!'

Kitty and Diggory sat on the bench together while Duke and the other cats set to work. Pixie scampered up and down the path, telling the other cats all about their garden rescue operation.

'Do you have any good ideas for your school garden design, Kitty?' said Pumpkin, jumping up beside her on the bench.

Kitty gazed around the sky garden. 'I'm definitely going to use recycled plant pots, and lots and lots of sunflowers!'

Pumpkin snuggled against her. 'What a busy night! I'm very sleepy now.'

Kitty smiled and yawned. 'Me too! But I'm so glad we had a new adventure and made some wonderful new friends!'

In the school garden.

Kitty's first sunflower.

Kitty, Pumpkin and Diggory.

Kitty's prize.

Kitty wins 1st prize.

Diggory ♡

About the author

Paula Harrison

Before launching a successful writing career,
Paula was a Primary school teacher. Her years teaching
taught her what children like in stories and how
they respond to humour and suspense. She went on
to put her experience to good use, writing many
successful stories for young readers.

About the illustrator

Jenny Løvlie

Jenny is a Norwegian illustrator, designer,
creative, foodie and bird enthusiast. She is fascinated
by the strong bond between humans and animals and
loves using bold colours and shapes in her work.

Love Kitty?
Why not try these too . . .

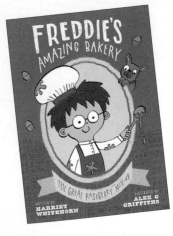